SONG LEE IN ROOM 2B

Twenty minutes later, it was time for the last person to speak. Miss Mackle tried to be casual about it. "Eh . . . let's see, Song Lee, I guess you're next."

Slowly, Song Lee got out of her seat. She walked up to the little wooden stand that sat on a desk and had a sign that said PODIUM.

Harry and I shook our heads. There was no way she was going to do this.

Song Lee took one look at the class and then ran out to the hallway.

I knew it!

Then something appeared in the doorway.

It was a big piece of cardboard that had a brown trunk, branches, lots of leaves, and a dozen pink Kleenex flowers.

"SONG LEE!" we all shouted as the tree moved across the classroom to the podium.

SONG LEE
IN ROOM 2B

BY SUZY KLINE
Pictures by Frank Remkiewicz

SCHOLASTIC INC.

New York Toronto London Auckland Sydney
Mexico City New Delhi Hong Kong

ISBN 0-439-15808-7

Text copyright © 1993 by Suzy Kline.
Illustrations copyright © 1993 by Frank Remkiewicz. All rights reserved.
Published by Scholastic Inc., 555 Broadway, New York, NY 10012,
by arrangement with Puffin Books, a division of
Penguin Putnam Inc. SCHOLASTIC and associated logos are
trademarks and/or registered trademarks of Scholastic Inc.

12 11 10 9 8 7 6 5 4 3 2   9/9 0 1 2 3 4/0

Printed in the U.S.A.   40

First Scholastic printing, September 1999

Set in Century Schoolbook

Dedicated with *love* to my class:

Amy Addison	Sara Hart
Krystal Avery	Phyllis Herrera
Christine Bascetta	Amy Hubbard
Scott Begey	Matthew Langin
Tanya Camire	Amorette Languell
Steven Caruso	Tara LaTulipe
Garrett Celadon	David Leisten
Joseph Conti	Gabrielle Lopez
Eric Crossman	Blake Paris
Yetzalee Cubero	Ricky Pestritto
Maria Fantasia	Patrick Reardon
Lisa Gelormino	Daniel Roberts
Guiseppe Graziano	Sarah Ruby
Roland Greenwood	Cynthia Twining

Contents

Shy Song Lee

Miss Mackle looked out the window of Room 2B. "It's snowing in March?"

Harry jumped out of his seat. "Hot dog! Come and see, Doug."

"All right!" I said, slapping Harry five. It was fun watching the snow stick to the playground and treetops.

When I turned around, everybody was up at the windows.

Except Song Lee.

The teacher smiled at her. "You have permission to leave your seat."

"Thank you, Miss Mackle."

Miss Mackle sighed. "I wish everyone in our second grade class had your good manners, Song Lee."

"STOP PUSHING!" Dexter shouted.

Harry held up a fist. "You're in my face. Move over, scuzzball."

Dexter put up two fists. "Make me, lizard breath."

"Harry and Dexter are fighting," Sidney called.

Miss Mackle waved her hands in the air. "That's it! Everyone sit down."

Harry and I shot Sidney a look. His tattling always got us in trouble.

After we returned to our seats, Miss Mackle looked at the class.

No one was smiling.

Most of us were moaning.

"I think we all have a case of cabin fever," Miss Mackle said.

"What's that?" Mary asked.

"It happens when people are cooped up in one place for a long time. Everyone gets grumpy."

"GGGGGrrrrr," Harry growled, as he stood up and dangled his arms like a monster.

Song Lee giggled.

"I wish I could fly this coop and go to Texas," I grumbled.

Miss Mackle snapped her fingers. "Doug, you just gave me an idea! It's time for Room 2B to take a vacation."

"YEAH!" we all shouted.

Mary counted the days on our bird calendar. "How can we? Spring break is two weeks away."

Miss Mackle held up the globe, and spun it once. "The mind can take you anywhere! For homework tonight, each one of you will prepare a talk, and take us to your favorite vacation spot. Tell us what it is like. Bring in family pictures, maps, or brochures if you have them."

"I never go anywhere," I groaned.

"Me, either," Sidney replied.

Song Lee raised her hand. She looked like she was going to cry.

"Yes?" Miss Mackle said.

"I feel sick."

I looked at Song Lee. She wasn't really sick. She just didn't want to stand in front of the class and give a talk.

Whenever the class had a play, Song Lee had a silent part, like a dead fish or Little Miss Muffet.

Miss Mackle put her hand on Song Lee's forehead. "You aren't warm. Is your stomach bothering you?"

Song Lee nodded. "I feel sick and sad all morning."

"Really? A moment ago you were giggling at Harry."

Song Lee looked down at her desk.

Miss Mackle patted her head. "Don't worry, Song Lee. You can give a short little talk tomorrow."

6

When the teacher left, Song Lee took out her pink cherry-blossom handkerchief.

"Are you crying?" I asked.

Song Lee sniffed a few times.

When she caught her breath she whispered, "If I don't give talk tomorrow, I get zero on homework chart."

"Don't worry," Harry said, putting his elbow on my desk. "You'll never have as many zeros as me."

I looked over at the homework chart. Song Lee's row of red stars was twice as long as Harry's. "Gee, you've *never* gotten a zero!"

Song Lee wiped her eyes. "I don't feel well. I stay home . . . write story about vacation. Mother bring story in and Miss Mackle give me red star on yellow homework chart."

"If you stay home, you'll miss my talk," I said.

"And *mine,*" Harry added, flashing his white teeth and making his thick eyebrows go up and down.

Song Lee giggled.

Harry could always make her laugh. Even now, when she had tears in her eyes.

"You *have* to come tomorrow," we said.

The next morning when the bell rang, Song Lee was not in her seat. The words PUBLIC SPEAKING were written on the board. By 9:30, five people had already talked about Disney World, Sea World, and Epcot Center. Lots of brochures were passed around. Posters and souvenirs were displayed on the chalkboard.

Sidney showed us some neat pictures of a barbecue on his back porch. He and his stepdad were wearing chef hats and cooking hamburgers.

When it was my turn, I put on Grampa's ten-gallon hat, got out Grandma's book about Texas, and started talking.

"I've never been to Texas but I'm going someday. Someday, I'm going to be the rootinest, the tootinest, and the shootinest cowboy ever to raise the dust on a high Texas plain."

When I was showing a picture of a

rodeo, Song Lee and her mother appeared at the door, so I stopped talking.

"Hello, Mrs. Park," the teacher said.

Song Lee was not smiling when she
dashed to her seat.

After Miss Mackle talked with Mrs.
Park in the hall, the teacher returned.
"Go on, Doug," she said.

So I did.

"You can visit the LBJ Ranch in
Texas. LBJ are initials for Lyndon
B. Johnson. He was president after
Kennedy was shot. This is a picture of
the Alamo."

Miss Mackle smiled when I sat down.
"I liked the way Doug had bookmarks
in his book to show us special places in
Texas. He was very organized. And his
hat was fun. Who would like to go
next?"

We all looked at Song Lee. She shook her head. "I . . . go . . . last."

"Harry?" Miss Mackle called.

Harry walked up to the front of the room with a souvenir book. I had seen it hundreds of times. It was about the House on the Rock in Wisconsin.

"You walk out on this long narrow beam and see the hills and trees below. Mom said it was creepy because the beam teetered. I thought it was fun."

Miss Mackle shivered. "You're . . . very brave, Harry."

Harry grinned.

Twenty minutes later, it was time for the last person to speak. Miss Mackle tried to be casual about it "Eh . . . let's see, Song Lee, I guess you're next."

Slowly, Song Lee got out of her seat. She walked up to the little wooden

stand that sat on a desk and had a sign
that said PODIUM.

Mary and Ida smiled at their friend.

Harry and I shook our heads. There
was no way she was going to do this.

Song Lee took one look at the class
and then ran out to the hallway.

I knew it!

Everyone looked at the teacher.

I thought she'd get mad. But she didn't. She just sat at the side of the room.

Waiting.

Then something appeared in the doorway.

It was a big piece of cardboard that had a brown trunk, branches, lots of leaves, and a dozen pink Kleenex flowers.

Harry and I pointed at the round holes that were cut out for eyes, nose, mouth, and hands.

"SONG LEE!" we all shouted as the tree moved across the classroom to the podium.

I stared at the two pink lips in the mouth-hole of the tree. They were beginning to move.

"I was born in Seoul, Korea . . . where Summer Olympics take place in 1988."

"Would the tree speak louder, please?" Miss Mackle said with a big smile.

When Song Lee nodded, the pink Kleenex flowers jiggled.

"Korea is size of Virginia. It is like Switzerland because it has many mountain and beautiful blue sky. There are many palace, royal tomb,

14

secret garden, and stone pagoda. We also have 3,000 island in Korea."

"Ooooh," the class replied.

Song Lee continued, "It is ten o'clock in Room 2B. In Korea, grandmother Bong sleep. It is midnight in Seoul."

Mary made some tally marks on a piece of paper. "Korea is 14 hours ahead of us!"

Song Lee shook the branches and made her green leaves and pink blossoms quiver. "In spring, we have many picnic under cherry tree at Korean park. My family play Ping-Pong and archery."

Harry stood up and shot a pretend arrow at Sidney. *"BOING!"*

Song Lee giggled. "It is time now for cherry-blossom tree to leave."

Everyone cheered as Song Lee

scooted outside to the hallway.

Miss Mackle went over to the yellow homework chart and added another star for Song Lee. This time it was a gold one!

As soon as Song Lee returned to her seat, she covered her face.

"Your talk was great!" I said.

Harry clapped. "You're the best tree in the world."

When she spread her fingers apart, I could see she was smiling.

I found out one thing about Song Lee that day. She may be shy, but she can sure surprise you.

Green with Envy

The next week it was St. Patrick's Day. Everyone in Room 2B was bringing something for our green smorgasbord.

As soon as Song Lee, Ida, and I got to class, we showed Miss Mackle what we brought.

"*Mmmmm,*" the teacher said, peeking inside the girls' plastic containers. "Lime jello and pistachio pudding! What did you bring, Doug?"

I couldn't wait to take off the plastic lid and show everyone. "Green eggs."

"GREEN EGGS?" they shouted.

"It was easy. Mom and I just peeled some hard-boiled eggs and colored them with green food coloring. I got the idea from Dr. Seuss."

Miss Mackle clapped her hands. "What fun! Well, I think you three should take these things downstairs to the cafeteria and ask Mrs. Funderburke if you can store them in the big refrigerator."

"Sure!" I said. It was exciting to get permission to go to the school kitchen.

Just then, Mary hurried into the classroom with a big box.

Miss Mackle smiled. "Goodness, Mary. What's in there?"

"Green cupcakes."

"Yum! They don't need refrigeration . . . do they?"

Mary shook her head.

"Then you won't need to go with Song Lee, Ida, and Doug."

Mary scowled as she leaned in the doorway and watched us walk down the hallway.

When we got to the kitchen, Mrs. Funderburke threw her hands in the air. "Oh, no! Not more green things!"

"Yes!" we replied.

"Let's see," the cook said, as she opened the big shiny chrome refrigerator door. "We already have grapes, green peppers, snap beans, Harry's ants . . ."

"ANTS?" Ida covered her mouth.

Mrs. Funderburke laughed. "Ants

are a delicacy. Harry has exquisite taste."

I made a face. I like to study ants but not *eat* them.

"Don't tell anyone," Mrs. Funderburke said. "Harry wanted his ants to be a surprise."

"We promise," Ida said, crossing her heart.

Song Lee crossed hers twice.

After we set our things carefully inside the big refrigerator, I smelled the air in the kitchen. "*Mmmmm.* What are you baking?"

"Oatmeal scotchies, Doug. Would you three like to sample one? They just came out of the oven."

"Yes!"

When Mrs. Funderburke handed us a warm cookie on a napkin, Song Lee softly said, "Thank you very much."

"Thank you very much," Ida and I copied.

When we got back to class, Mary was waiting for us at the door. "What took you so long?"

I licked some butterscotch off my lips. "We got a cookie. A warm one right out of the oven."

"No fair!" Mary replied.

"We also heard a secret from the cook," Ida said.

Song Lee gave us a look. I could tell she was disappointed. Ida and I were making Mary feel left out.

"What secret?"

"We can't tell," Ida said.

Mary put her hands on her hips. "You shouldn't keep secrets. We're friends!"

"We crossed our hearts," Ida replied. Then Ida and I went over and admired the green smorgasbord. Someone had just brought in green sugar cookies, a jar of pickles, and green-onion potato chips.

When I looked back at Mary, she was steaming mad! She just glared at Song Lee in the seat next to her. "You better tell me that secret or else."

Song Lee took a piece of paper out of her desk and drew a shamrock. Then she wrote a message inside with green crayon.

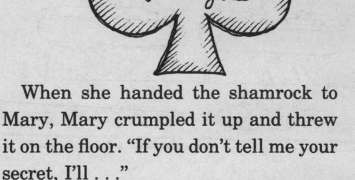

When she handed the shamrock to Mary, Mary crumpled it up and threw it on the floor. "If you don't tell me your secret, I'll . . ."

Just then the bell rang, and Miss

Mackle greeted the class. "Happy St. Patrick's Day, boys and girls."

Everyone said "Happy St. Patrick's Day" back, except Mary.

"We'll have our green smorgasbord after lunch," the teacher said. "But right now, we're going to read from the *greenest* story in literature!"

"What's the title?" Ida asked.

"You all know it."

"We do?"

"Does it have green slime in it?" Harry asked.

Miss Mackle rolled her eyeballs, sat down in her reading chair, and opened a book.

"*THE WIZARD OF OZ!*" we all shouted.

"Right! And now it's time to follow the yellow brick road to the Emerald

City where *everything* is green."

We all got comfortable while Miss Mackle began reading about Dorothy, the Scarecrow, the Tin Man, and the Cowardly Lion.

Mary even forgot how angry she was. For one hour.

When the teacher closed her book, we just sat there. I don't think any of us wanted to leave the Emerald City.

Miss Mackle walked over to the tall cabinet, took out some green clay, and broke off a piece for each person. "Now, how about making some miniature characters?"

"Yeah!" we replied.

When Sidney got his lump of clay, he used the whole thing to make a dog. "Ta-dah! It's Toto!" Then he barked for a while.

Song Lee was shaping a little ax for her tiny Tin Man.

"That's great," I said.

"It's mean," Mary said. "You're keeping a secret. I bet it's about me."

Song Lee shook her head. "It is not secret about you. It is . . . secret about . . . Harry."

Mary looked over at Harry. He was putting a wart on the Wicked Witch of the West.

"What about him?" Mary asked.

"It is surprise. I cannot tell," Song Lee said.

"If you don't tell me, I'll . . ." Mary squeezed her clay so hard, it oozed through her fingers like long green snakes.

Then it happened.

Mary did something really awful.

She raised her hand and mashed a clump of clay on Song Lee's head.

A second later Miss Mackle looked up. "Song Lee! Who put that clay in your hair?"

Mary turned away.

"I did," Song Lee said. "It is St. Patrick's Day hat."

"Are you sure?"

"Yes."

We all knew Song Lee just didn't want to tattle.

"Hmmm," the teacher said. "You know we don't put clay in our hair."

"Yes, Miss Mackle." And she pulled it off her head.

I looked over at Mary. She was wiping her eyes with her sweater sleeve. "I'm sorry, Song Lee," she whispered. "You are the nicest person I know."

That afternoon, when it was time for our green smorgasbord, we all lined up. Harry was first. Mr. Cardini, the principal, was second. And I was third. Song Lee was holding hands with Mary and Ida behind me.

Everyone watched Harry uncover his plastic container. "Ta-dah! ANTS!"

"ANTS?" everyone gasped.

Then Harry showed us what was inside. Twenty-four small pieces of celery filled with peanut butter and dotted with raisins.

"Ants on a log," Harry replied, biting into one. "*Deeeee*-licious." When he made the peanut butter ooze between his teeth, all of us groaned.

Except Song Lee.

She couldn't stop giggling.

Song Lee's Nosebook

The next morning, I looked up at the classroom clock. We had 15 minutes to write in our notebooks. What could I write about? Miss Mackle said write about anything.

My mind was a blank.

I looked out the window and stared at the snow on the tree branches.

Then I looked at our terrarium.

Three sick plants in an old fish tank.

When I got up and looked inside, I noticed some grayish-green mold growing in one corner.

"Sit down, Doug," Miss Mackle said.

When I returned to my seat, I looked over at Harry. He was writing. He was also blowing his nose with a Kleenex.

"What should I write about?" I whispered.

"*SHHHHH!*" Harry said.

It was no use talking to him now. He was in his own little world.

Miss Mackle was busy writing in her notebook in front of the room. I wondered what she was writing. I liked what she wrote yesterday. It was about a summer picnic when three yellow jackets attacked her cupcake.

"*Bzzzz!*" I pretended to be a wasp flying in the room. "*Bzzzz! Bzzzz!*"

"*Shhhh!*" Ida said.

"*SHHHH!*" Harry said.

I stopped buzzing.

What was *I* going to write about?

Five minutes later, when Miss Mackle called everyone up to the sharing circle, I still had a blank page.

Harry was still writing.

"I've got three pages!" Ida said.

"I've got six!" Harry bragged.

I moved my chair next to Song Lee. She just had one page.

Ida read first. "Last Saturday, I went over to Song Lee's house. Mary came, too. We played lots of games and had lunch. Mrs. Park made us *kimchi*. That is Korean. It has red peppers and cabbage and other vegetables in it. After lunch we played some more. The day was very, very, very, very—"

By the time she turned the page, Miss Mackle stopped her. "Ida, you have written two more pages of *very*'s?"

"Yes." Then she continued reading. ". . . very, very, very, very—"

When everyone started laughing, the teacher asked, "It was very *what?*"

Ida turned the page and read the last word. "Fun."

Miss Mackle smiled. "I loved the part about the *kimchi,* but one *very* is enough."

Ida made a face. She wanted to read her two pages of *very*'s.

Harry read next. "Yesterday, I went to Antarctica and fed two penguins . . ."

We all leaned forward. It was another one of Harry's great adventures in the wild. By the time he got to the fifth

page, an iceberg crashed on his head and he was squished like a bug.

Everyone started clapping when Harry finished.

"That's quite an ending!" Miss Mackle said. "Squished like a bug!"

Harry flashed a toothy smile.

Then the teacher looked at me. "Doug? Will you read what you wrote?"

"I couldn't think of anything. I don't have Harry's imagination."

Miss Mackle nodded. "That's called writer's block. It happens to everyone. I still want to hear from you, though, Doug. Let me know when you get an inspiration."

"What's an inspiration?" I asked.

"It gives you an idea," the teacher said. "It hits you like a flash."

"I'll wait for that flash, then," I said.

Miss Mackle smiled. "Song Lee?"

Song Lee didn't mind reading aloud in the sharing circle. It wasn't like she was standing in front of an audience. She just held her notebook up high so no one could see her face.

As soon as she read the title, everyone laughed.

"Harry's Nose.

"I notice Harry has cold today. Four times, he blow his nose into white Kleenex. Now, skin around Harry's nose is red and crusty. His nostril must be very sore. I feel sad for Harry's nose."

When she finished, Harry was smiling. Everyone could tell he liked the story.

"That's gross," said Sidney.

"I like it!" Miss Mackle replied. "Writers notice lots of things. Things that are beautiful and things that are not so beautiful, like . . . Harry's nose."

Just then it hit me. I grabbed my pencil and started writing.

Ten minutes later when everyone had shared, I raised my hand. "I'm ready."

"Doug! You don't have writer's block anymore?"

"No. Song Lee's story gave me an idea."

"Sounds like an *inspiration!*" Miss Mackle said.

"Yeah! Now *I* want to write about something *I* noticed."

Dexter rubbed his hands together. "Is it about Harry's boogers?"

As soon as we burst out laughing, Miss Mackle changed the subject. "Does your story have a title, Doug?"

I nodded.

"*Murder in Room 2B.*"

Suddenly, everyone turned quiet.

I waited a moment before I began to read.

"Green fuzz grows in our terrarium. I saw it in one corner. It has little gray hairs. It is like a monster creeping toward our three sick plants. If we don't stop it, there will be murder in Room 2B!"

When I looked up from my notebook, the teacher's face was red. She was also sinking down in her chair. "Class, I think I know where that grayish-green fuzz is coming from."

We all stared at Miss Mackle.

"Where?"

"Well, sometimes when I'm in a

hurry, I dump my leftover coffee into the terrarium."

"*Ee-yew!*" we said.

"I guess the milk and sugar must be getting moldy. I didn't realize what it was doing to the soil until Doug read from his notebook today."

Harry put his hands up. "Oh, no! Our teacher is a *Coffee Monster*."

When Miss Mackle started laughing, we did, too.

"Boys and girls," she said. "I promise never to dump coffee in there again.

Doug's story is a good example of how writing *can* make a difference. Now our plants are saved from the Coffee Monster!"

While everyone cheered and clapped, I just leaned back in my chair and smiled. I really felt like a writer today.

"Thanks, Song Lee," I said. "I got my inspiration from you and your nose-book. I mean notebook."

"Nosebook!" Song Lee giggled. "That is funny. Now you give me inspiration, Doug."

Then she took out a Magic Marker and drew a picture of a nose with two nostrils on the cover of her notebook.

Song Lee and Chungju

Monday morning, Harry and I looked at the lunch menu. "PIZZA!" we said, slapping each other five. Then we walked over to the monitor chart.

"Hot dog!" Harry said. "I'm Sweeper, and you're Plant Monitor, Doug."

"All right! I get to water our three sick plants."

Song Lee looked confused when she read the chart. Ant Monitor and Fish Monitor were crossed off, and in their place was Science Monitor. That's what she was. "Miss Mackle," she said, "what does Science Monitor do?"

"Well, you know the ants died off because we didn't have a queen ant, and over the holidays, I gave away our three goldfish to children in our class who have tanks."

"Yes?"

"So, now . . . the Science Monitor just keeps the science corner neat."

Song Lee put her head down. "We have no living thing in our room anymore?"

"We have 22 children and three sick

plants that are getting better!" Miss Mackle exclaimed.

"No living thing," Song Lee said sadly.

The next day, when Song Lee came to class, she was carrying a small box and a bag of stuff.

Miss Mackle greeted her at the door. "What do we have here?"

"A salamander. I name him Chungju after city in Korea."

Miss Mackle's eyes widened as she watched Song Lee take the salamander out of the box and put him into a deep blue bowl that was filled with mud and one big rock.

"Hello, Chungju!"

Lots of people crowded around the science table. "Neat-o!" I said, as Harry and I shared a chair in front of the bowl.

Ida and Mary rushed into the classroom. *"Ohhhhhh!"* Mary exclaimed. "A
salamander!"

"Ee-yew," Sidney groaned. "I bet that salamander slithers out of the bowl, slides down the table leg, slithers over to someone's desk, slithers up their pants, slithers across their stomach, slithers up their neck, and . . ."

"SIDNEY!" Mary said. "Stop slithering! I don't need any nightmares."

"Don't worry, Mary," Song Lee said. "Chungju can't get out. I have him for one year. He is fine in bowl."

"One year! Wow!" I said.

Harry scooted our chair closer to Song Lee's. "Remember when you brought in Bong, your water frog? How is he doing?"

"He is fine." After Song Lee talked about Bong for a while, Harry stood up and shouted, "HE'S GONE! CHUNGJU ESCAPED!"

Sidney jumped so high he knocked the bird mobile down. "Help!" he called as he tried to untangle the toucan and the lovebird from his hair.

"April fool," Harry said. "Chungju is behind the rock."

Sidney gritted his teeth. "It's not

April Fools' Day, ol' Harry the canary. It's still March!"

"Just practicing," Harry replied, as he flashed a big smile.

"What's going on?" Miss Mackle asked.

Before the teacher could get to our table, the fire alarm went off. It was loud and shrill. *ENNH! ENNH! ENNH!*

Miss Mackle turned off the lights. *"Line up, single file. No running.* Sidney, we'll take care of that mess in your hair later. *Class, follow me!"*

Quickly, we did exactly what the teacher said. We made one straight line, followed her down the hall, and out the front doors of South School. As soon as we got outside, I could see my breath in the cold air.

Harry crunched the snow as he stomped ahead of me. "Neat-o! A fire drill!"

"This is no drill," Mary scolded. "I bet the school's on fire!"

"No way," I said. "It's just practice."

"No, it isn't!" Mary replied. "We never practice when it's cold. This time it's for real!"

When we stopped at the telephone pole around the corner, Miss Mackle started counting heads.

"LOOK!" Sidney shouted, as he flipped the lovebird over his head.

"THREE FIRE ENGINES!"

Everyone watched the shiny red engines roar up the road and screech to a halt in front of the school. Mary plugged her ears. Ida rubbed her arms. "I've got goose bumps," she said.

"THERE THEY GO!" Harry yelled, as we watched the fire fighters with their big black boots jump off the trucks and run up the steps of South School.

Miss Mackle was still counting heads. When she finished, she looked worried. "Only 21? Someone's missing!"

We all looked at each other.

"Where's Song Lee?" Harry said.

"SONG LEE!" we shouted.

Miss Mackle quickly asked a nearby teacher to watch our class, then she rushed back to the school.

Harry and I stared at the brick building and waited. No one said anything.

Except Sidney.

"She's probably burnt to a crisp right now."

"Sidney!" Mary groaned.

Harry held up a fist.

I stood on my toes and could see Miss Mackle talking to the sixth-grade teacher in the front of the line. He was telling her something.

"Where is Song Lee?" Mary and Ida moaned as they huddled together.

Harry was biting his nails.

I kept my eyes on the teacher. She was making her way back to our line. When she got close, we could see she had her arm around someone.

"SONG LEE!" we yelled.

Song Lee had a sweater wrapped around her blue bowl.

"CHUNGJU! CHUNGJU!" we chanted.

Song Lee had saved her salamander!

While we were chanting "CHUNG-JU" for the third time, Mr. Cardini appeared on the front steps and raised his hand.

We turned pin quiet.

"One pepperoni pizza burned in the oven and set off the alarm in the school kitchen. It's okay now!"

Everyone laughed as we hurried into the building. Harry and I waved at the fire fighters.

When we got back to Room 2B, it felt nice and warm. Miss Mackle talked to us as soon as we sat down.

"Song Lee took an extra minute to get her sweater and wrap it around Chungju's bowl. That extra minute separated her from our class. She ended up following the sixth graders out of the building. But now she knows how important our rule is about staying together during a fire drill."

"I bet the fire fighters would have saved Chungju," Harry said.

"Next time I stay with class," said Song Lee, as she set the bowl down on the science table.

"Good," the teacher said. "Now, how is Chungju doing?"

"He doesn't like fire drill," Song Lee said. "He hide under mud."

"Hey, what about me?" Sidney called. "I still have lovebirds in my hair!"

Harry patted him on the back. "We always knew you were a birdbrain, Sidney!"

Miss Mackle tried not to laugh as she began untangling the mobile on Sidney's head.

While the class watched the teacher,

I looked over at Song Lee.

She was talking to a bowl of mud.

"Come on out, Chungju! It is warm and safe now."

After two long minutes, a head popped out.

Song Lee's smile was as big as Texas. Or I *should* say, Korea.

Song Lee. Most of the time, she follows the rules. But when she doesn't, it's because she follows her heart.